# THE
# LION KING
## A DAY WITHOUT
## PUMBAA

THIS BOOK BELONGS TO:

_____

# THE
# LION KING
## A DAY WITHOUT
## PUMBAA

Written by Lara Bergen
Illustrated by Manuela Razzi and Andrea Cagol

DISNEP PRESS

Los Angeles • New York

Adapted from the story originally published in the book *5-Minute Stories: Friendship*, written by Augusto Macchetto and Paola Mulazzi. Copyright © 2005 Disney Enterprises, Inc.

For information address Disney Press, 1200 Grand Central Avenue, Glendale, California 91201.
ISBN 978-1-368-04874-3
FAC-023680-19152

Printed in China
First Box Set Edition, June 2019
1 3 5 7 9 10 8 6 4 2

For more Disney Press fun, visit www.disneybooks.com

"**M**mm!" said Timon the meerkat. "Breakfast time! Come to Daddy, you tasty little critters."

Timon was showing Simba the lion cub how to catch some very sneaky bugs in the jungle.

"Too bad Pumbaa has to miss out on this feast," Timon remarked. "I haven't seen him since sunup. Have you? *Ooh!* There's a good one! Watch me, Simba—and learn!"

Timon crouched behind a rotten log crawling with beetles. He was about to pounce, when—

*"AAAHHH!"* Without any warning, Pumbaa swooped out of the trees, swinging wildly on a vine. He plowed straight into Timon, flattening the meerkat like a pancake.

"Oops! Sorry, Timon," Pumbaa said, picking himself up.

*"Sorry?"* shouted Timon. *"Sorry,* you say? That's the nineteenth—no, the *twentieth* time you've crashed into me this week!"

"But it wasn't on purpose," Pumbaa told him.

"You never do anything on purpose," Timon replied. "You're a *natural* disaster! Why, you couldn't catch a bug if it flew into your mouth."

"That's not true!" Pumbaa protested, tears welling up in his eyes. "Look! I'll prove it."

The clumsy warthog lunged for a juicy grub, only to fall headfirst into a puddle. Mud splattered Simba and Timon.

"That's it!" cried Timon. "I've had it! No more disasters!"

Pumbaa looked heartbroken. "Do you think I'm a disaster, too?" he asked Simba.

"Well," Simba replied, "you have to admit, sometimes you do things that *are* pretty disastrous."

Pumbaa hung his head. "You're right," he said. "Nobody wants me around. It would be better for everyone if I just left."

With that, Pumbaa slowly plodded off into the jungle.

Just then, the clouds thickened, and a bolt of lightning shot through the sky.

"Wait a second," said Simba, looking up at the threatening clouds. "Timon, we can't let him go!"

But Timon wouldn't even turn to watch his friend leave. "If that warthog thinks I'm going to beg him to stay, he's sorely mistaken," Timon said. "Trust me, Simba, he'll be back by lunchtime."

But as rain began to pour down, Simba wasn't so sure.

The storm came and went. And then so did lunchtime—but still, no Pumbaa. Simba began to worry.

Simba looked off in the direction Pumbaa had gone.

"We shouldn't have been so hard on him," the little cub said. "I wonder if he's okay."

"He's fine," snapped Timon, who was still sore from getting squashed that morning. "Besides, he's the one who walked out on us, remember? *Poof!* Gone! History, as far as I'm concerned. Pumbaa? Who's that? Never heard of him!"

Simba sighed.

"Oh, stop moping," Timon said. "And think about it. We can do anything we want now—without worrying about getting knocked down, covered with mud, or run over. Let's enjoy it."

As Timon marched off, Simba followed behind.

First, Simba and Timon tried chasing vultures. Then, they splashed in the river. They even tried playing a game of tag among the vines. But somehow, nothing they did seemed like very much fun. Something—or *someone*—was always missing.

"So, what do you want to do now?" Timon asked Simba.

"I don't know," replied Simba. "What do *you* want to do?"

"I asked you first," said Timon.

The sun began to dip below the horizon. Timon sighed. He was bored. And, he admitted to himself, it was also possible that he missed Pumbaa—just a little.

By the time Simba and Timon finished dinner, they were both a little grumpy. They hadn't really enjoyed anything they'd done that day. Soon it would be bedtime, and their friend still hadn't returned.

"There's got to be something fun to do," said Simba.

"Well," Timon said gloomily, "what do *you* want to do?"

"I don't know," said Simba. "What do *you* want to do?"

The pair went on . . . and on . . . and on. They would have gone on even longer, but suddenly they heard a rustling sound coming from along the riverbank.

"Timon! Simba! Look what I found!"

*Wham!* Pumbaa tumbled out of the jungle, knocking into Timon and Simba. All three of them crashed into the trunk of a large tree. Pumbaa had brought bugs for his friends, but the critters went flying into the air.

"I'm back," Pumbaa said with a groan. The fall had hurt a little.

"So we see," mumbled Timon, trapped under the warthog. Embarrassed, Pumbaa stood up and faced his friends. "I came back to say I missed you," he said. "But now look what I've done! I'm the worst friend ever." Pumbaa started to walk sadly back into the jungle.

"Now, wait one minute!" cried Timon. "That's just not true!"

"You're a wonderful friend, and we missed you!" Simba said. "We even missed your disasters," he added.

Pumbaa stopped and looked at his friends hopefully.

"It appears," Timon said with a small smile, "that we've grown accustomed to being stepped on, bruised, and squashed."

"You mean you're willing to put up with me?" Pumbaa asked, trying to hold back happy tears.

"You bet!" Simba exclaimed. "You're our very favorite disaster."

Pumbaa rushed toward them. As he did, he accidentally knocked over Timon and stepped on Simba's paw. But this time his friends didn't really mind.

As Simba curled up to sleep, he was already looking forward to the adventures that lay in store the next day—with both his friends!